VIKING STUDIO

Published by the Penguin Group, Penguin Putnam Inc.,
375 Hudson Street, New York, New York 10014, U.S.A.
Penguin Books Ltd, 27 Wrights Lane, London W8 5TZ, England
Penguin Books Australia Ltd, Ringwood, Victoria, Australia
Penguin Books Canada Ltd, 10 Alcorn Avenue,
Toronto, Ontario, Canada M4V 3B2
Penguin Books (N.Z.) Ltd, 182-190 Wairau Road,
Auckland 10, New Zealand

Penguin Books Ltd, Registered Offices:
Harmondsworth, Middlesex, England

First American Edition published in 2000 by Viking Studio,
a member of Penguin Putnam Inc.

1 2 3 4 5 6 7 8 9 10

Copyright © Rafiq Abdulla, 2000
Notes on the poems written by Mehri Niknam © Frances Lincoln Ltd, 2000
Details about the manuscripts written by Tim Stanley © Frances Lincoln Ltd, 2000
Copyright © Frances Lincoln Ltd, 2000

All rights reserved

ISBN 0-670-88935-0

CIP data available

Printed in China

Set in Baker Signet

Words of Paradise

SELECTED POEMS OF RUMI

New Interpretations by Raficq Abdulla

Illustrated with Persian and Islamic Manuscripts

VIKING STUDIO

To Adam & Marianne for keeping my feet

on the ground, which is where we all begin . . .

– R. A.

TO MAULANA RUMI

Poet – first a seeker of Truth
Then a lover torn from the glove
Of your passion; you learnt to
Speak from the heart, your voice
Like the unlettered prophet intoned
Miracles. Your sun was more fiery
Earth then fire and bound to die
When his work was done. Suffering
Was the black work of his absence,
It seduced you into visions lighting
The landscape of memory – a man
Made new with each whirling second.
Your words conscript generations,
With you, God ceased to be a cliché,
He had come to pluck the diamond
Of himself from your burgled heart.

- R. A.

Introduction

Why do we read the poems of Jalaluddin Rumi today? He is a man from a different time and a different culture, a mystic, an Islamic scholar of the 13th century CE who wrote in Persian. What is it about the poems that make us read them time and again? Why do we feel a thrill of recognition reading them 700 years after they were written?

I believe the secret lies in the quality of lived experience, the intense yearning or desire for something greater than ourselves, something which emanates power, awe, love and beauty (one of the ninety-nine names of God in the Islamic tradition is Jamal which means beauty). It is the feeling of homecoming in a world in which we are displaced, un-rooted, that is the essence of Rumi's verse and what draws us to it. Of course, there is more to Rumi's poetry. It is filled with great wisdom and passion, like so much mystical or spiritual verse. It moves with an erotic energy, something akin to what the writer Rolande Barthes has called *jouissance* – an orgasmic, joyous quality that grabs and revitalizes us, even though it speaks of longing and loss.

Reading Rumi's poetry is like making love. We should be ready to lose ourselves in it, as only then will we find the Other, that greater energy which contains us. Rumi wrote poetry not only to be read in the silent privacy of the mind, but to be listened to with other like-minded people, as we listen to a symphony, and move with its music. It's no wonder that Rumi was the founder of the whirling dervishes, as he understood that true ecstasy – the feeling of transcending one's physical and spiritual limitations – occurs paradoxically through movement of the body which opens new levels of awareness in the consciousness. There is no mind/body division in Rumi's world view. Everything is in flux, flowing constantly from one situation to another; everything is a manifestation of the Divine, emanations transmitted like light from the sun through our solar system. We are particles in orbit around this wonderful source of power and love – this sun – longing to return to it, to be annihilated by it and discover our true nature. Rumi's verse exemplifies this mercurial quality of loss, longing and love – we always look for completion, and the only true completion we find is in losing ourselves in the Beloved.

Most of the poems selected in this book come from two major sources: the *Divan* to Shams-e Tabriz and the *Mathnavi-e Ma'navi*. The *Divan* is the collection of lyrical odes to the inspirational and controversial figure of Shams-e Tabriz. He came into Rumi's life unbidden, and turned it upside down by his presence and secret teachings. When he disappeared as mysteriously as he had come, his absence almost drove Rumi out of his mind. However, through a process of personal transformation, Rumi's love for Shams was transfigured into the Beloved, the leitmotif for the Divine.

The *Mathnavi-e Ma'navi* or *Poem of Inner Meanings* runs for thousands of verses and is made up of countless interweaving stories, interspersed with more generalized observations. In this great didactic work, Rumi attempts to describe every aspect of mystical perception and aspiration. The *Mathnavi* is so highly regarded in the Muslim world that it has been audaciously called the Qur'an in Persian.

Unfortunately, as most of us are unable to enjoy the musicality and outflowing energy of Rumi's poetry in the original Persian, we try to capture it in translations, or transpositions and interpretations, in languages we can understand. There is no such thing as an exact translation unless it is the translation of the reader or listener who reads the source text fluently. This may be possible with contemporary texts but, I believe, it is not possible with poetry from other historical periods which inevitably was written for, and understood by, readers with different expectations and values. In such cases, we are not only reading a text from a remote period which catered to people who are long dead, but the significance of the poem in its context has also passed away irrevocably. We may only guess at it. More importantly, we can re-create the poetry in our own idiom. This is a tricky business – and in bridging the cultural, linguistic, and chronological gulf between the original and its modern re-creation, I have not shied away from radical departures from a 'literal' understanding of translation, in order to convey that part of the original's spirit that most clearly speaks to the modern reader. I have tried to interpret these poems of Rumi, threading the maze of their meaning and language into a contemporary idiom whilst keeping the original energy, tension, eclectic imagery and lucidity of Rumi's verse. I have endeavoured to retain the significance of the spiritual concepts he used, making them more accessible to the modern Western reader. Inevitably we are confronted with deviations of form and language, but my aim was to come closer to the feel and lyrical intention of the original. I want to convey something of the beauty and intensity of Rumi's language and imagery whilst keeping us close to some of his spiritual insights which, after all, are the kernel of what attracts us to his poetry in the first place.

Rumi wrote poetry to transform his listeners and readers, to take them out of themselves, to make them drunk with the Divine. In this disenchanted age where we float aimlessly in a sort of postmodern irreality, where images cheat us of a sense of ourselves, Rumi has something important to say to all of us. His poetry lights a fire in us, something incandescent with longing to attain greater levels of awareness in ourselves, to break out of the mould of our solitude to a greater, life-enhancing whole.

Music opens our hearts and surely ensnares
With echoes that spill from celestial spheres;
And faith far beyond the impaled cast of thought
Turns ugly dissonance to honey by angels brought.

Adam's children tuned and so coarsely tied
Hear with him the angels' songs and smiling sigh.
We remember them, even faintly, as yearning
Heartbeats of the sweet soul's original learning.

Oh, music feeds the calling souls of lovers,
Music raises the spirit from its earthly covers.
The ashes grow bolder and shed their fur
Listen with stillness that only souls can share.

Mathnavi IV, 733

Dawn – conceived light: the pregnant moon
Rises concave into the blood-streamed sky
Casting off the face of fading night.
Hovering over my uplifted eyes,
It showers me with legendary silver,
Then like a falcon hunting its prey
It swoops down to take me in its talons and rise,
Rise again in a great signature curve naming God,
High into the breaking sky.
My soul in flight straining gravity sees naught
Save the mythic eye of the moon which fills
My paltry body with the cool grace of silver light
Refining the unlettered soul from dross; it grows
Tenderly transparent with the teeming height,
Transparent as the mercy of flowing water;
Polished by the fire of Being – felt not spoken –
Until the lens of my unskinned soul
Opening to the Void, is carelessly dissolved.

Divan 649

Now that your soul has entered my all-too-present flesh
And made with it a soul in kind,
Your each embarking thought,
The breathing swing and sway of your every movement
Makes an impression on the wax of my surrendering will.
My mind is but a pillow
Indented by the flow of your passing thoughts.
My newly-moulded soul is alight with
Your pulsing grace, your secret deceptions
Have transformed dead stone to fire.
Each new day is a slow beginning,
New lamentations rise
From the reed of my longing for your lip;
Your loving candour strokes the mouth of the reed
With a sweet languishing refrain.
My soul imitates and installs
Your moon's soft milk-light in its chambers.
I mould myself to fit your form
Like a belt for the waist, even when
Your eye has tethered me with angry scowls
Turning me this way and that until
My distracted heart jumps out of itself.

Divan 2313

I gaze at the porcelain of your face and my heart lights up,
Your gentle nature teaches me to float into your embrace;
And then your laughter, it draws from me
A sequence of joy; my musk and distilled rose
Make vintage of your cunning scent.
Your secret moon is my emblem,
Your hair my shaded bower.
I place my forehead on the dust of your entrance,
I leap with eagerness into that place of yours
Where lights play only on your chosen guest.
There is no pole for my heart other
Than the pull from your direction.
Even if this heart is disarrayed by others,
It is returned to its keeper,
That connecting wholeness that is yourself.
I am tossed and bewildered

By the secret river of your being which
Induces me in its sweet current.
I plunge like a salmon with desperate, bucking energy
To test your flow. Your breasts,
As soft as the moon's dreaming light,
Turn me to gold as your sacred fold entrances me,
Incubates my desire and makes us one.
Why should my head which presses you with
Tender burning, not rest itself against your precious
Central place and wait to be struck by your mallet?
No, it's time I learnt to be silent; yes, silent,
Since my savage moans of love
Are bisected and broken into meagre whimpering
By your own despatching cry.

Divan 2253

Seated here attached to the present of this royal place
We are a singing joy, you and I.
Two in form two in figure, two to the outward eye
We're one in one, you and I.
The grove's verdant green picked in birdsong
Treats us kindly with a trace of eternity
As we enter the garden, you and I.
The unnumbered eyes of the stars gaze on us,
We turn on them the moon's face, you and I.
You and I, refined with joy, more than you and I
Set apart from the dross of empty words, you and I,
We are, you in I and I in you, the envy of gorgeous
Birds of paradise when we melt in secret laughter,
You and I, the mystery is you and I as we sit
Together in this royal place, yet in this cusp
Of being in the shade of common bliss we are one
You and I,
You and I,
We are at once in Iraq and Khorasan
You and I.

Divan 322

And this is Love – the vertigo of heaven
Beyond the cage of words,
Suddenly to be naked in the searchlight
Of truth, no shade no leaf for the senses.
You are a victim, Love's felony pillages your breath
Knocks away your feet, makes you blind with insight,
So that you may clearly see for yourself.
Congratulate your heart whilst you can, for it has
Clambered into the inner chamber of circling lovers;
Now it sees with uncluttered eye and rashly
Enters the rough neighbourhood of loving breasts.
What is the origin of your energy, O heart?
Where is the drastic home of your pulse?
Birds may sing their busy language
I shall hear them with a lover's newfound ear!
The heart complains: "I was in travail
As the body was burnt. I fled the workshop
Even as it was being made. When I was exhausted
Beaten down, I was dragged through madness beyond
Description, torn apart beyond the good sense of sounds."

Divan 1919

I am you and you are me, you in me, me in you,
Oh Beloved, do not wander from your longing breast,
Oh Beloved, do not think you're estranged from me,
Do not Beloved, do not exile yourself from home.
Do not Oh Beloved, do not taunt my head, don't tempt
My foot so I become a fool who stamps his cruel heel
Upon his broken head. I'm fired with you Oh Beloved,
I flow from you as your leaning shadow; you cannot,
My Beloved, plunge your dagger into this shadow of yours.
Cherish this dancing darkness like a tree nurses its own,
Letting it sway from the founding path of its trunk.
Bring all the shadows into the sun of your eye so they
Will merge in the light of your cheek. My heart's domain
Is disordered by your distance, torn with civil strife;
Mount your throne Oh Beloved, remain in charge.
"Reason is the crown" the Caliph Ali said
With the emancipation of a poet; now take from your grace
Oh Beloved, place on your throne a new diamond
Mined from the shadow of your being.

Divan 1254

Where is he?
Where is my soul's delight?
My North, my West, my South and East?
He's not here amongst you who conceive nothing.
Where has he gone?
He is not here, not here,
Not even the compassing aroma of his presence
Dwells amongst you who receive nothing.
I look here, I look there,
I look up and down,
I cannot see even the shadow of his beard.
Oh believers, speak to me!
Tell me where he has gone who shone
Like a blue flame in my conceiving eye.

Shout out his name and your echoing bones
Shall never crumble in the receiving grave.
You who have kissed his hand are blessed,
Even in death your lips shall remain sweet as melons.
Should I be grateful for the incomparable beauty of his face
Or for the sweet severity of his demeanour?
Even if his lucid soul is no longer sketched
In the memory of his body, it does not matter;
My Love revolves like the planets around the storm of his Sun.
Call out for Shams, my soul requires him,
Chant his familiar names of friendship,
Lighten the gravity of our grief,
Enliven the ear's lassitude with the energy of his name.

Divan 1235

Last night your dreams blindfolded
You with light. Tonight, you're
Incomplete, moving and turning
Like an eel in the pool of my back;
I say in fabled whispers: "You and I
Will be one with one, you and I
Till the world returns to the One.

You groan and sigh, and smile
In sleep saying things that rise
So deep from the cup of Love.

Ruba'iyat 1879

Where you dwell is dear to my sight
A celestial city bedecked in light.
In whatever corner you are found
Small as a needle's eye, is holy ground.
Wherever the rainbow of your face alights
Be it the dank gorge of a well, it's paradise.
With your presence in hell a heaven is discerned
The rigour of prison to a lover's garden is turned.
The Devil's chamber with you glows with delight,
Your absence makes beauty horror, widowing my sight.

Mathnavi III, 3808

Each of My creatures has its own path
Each way to worthy each is in My gift;
Hardness of heart plucks each from the hearth,
You are My servant whose words should uplift
All who hear you and receive My message.
I am not labour to be lost in the fickle passage
Of a fine tongue and splendid speech, there's more
Much more I seek for My creature's prayer to be sure.
It is the spirit and the spring of inner feeling,
The innocence of heart that sorely beseeches the Lord
Which knows not clever language, but appealing
From his centre My creature finds always the words
Untainted by conceit and its siblings but fired with Love.
Words born of bereavement, conceived from burning
Burning, burning which rises up like thirst above
The carcass of thought and fine speech, freshly turning
Their faces to Me in their simple, heart-felt yearning.
Remember, Moses, the supplicant who sets his heart
In forms is a shadow; the soul which burns to be a part
Of the Greater is the living heart within the encrusted form
Of prayer, which cries out constantly to be taken by storm.

The religion of the heart is not a stark monument of stone;
Lovers of God have no religion save yearning for Me alone.

Mathnavi II, 1750

How close are these two immaterial things – my soul to your soul!
Telepathy is the way we astonish each other in our paradise.
But we are even closer than that, come nearer so that the surface
Of our questing souls may co-mingle like wisps of sea-mist.
Come nearer, don't jest and say with soft irony: "I am a dervish
In your midst". Our conjunction is not so simply told as that.
I am the pillar which holds up the ceiling, I am the gutter collecting
Rain water from the roof, I am your salty conscience on Judgement Day;
Don't take me as the oil of passing acquaintances without history.
I am the wine at your banquet, the proud and terrible lance of your battles.
If like lightning I suddenly pierce the dark bulk of night then go out;
I am also the blinding electricity of your beauty, clean, silent and lethal.
I am an ocean of joy, so drunk I take and give soul for soul without

Quibbling pedantry between your heaven and my earth. You make
Blossom in me worlds as numerous as atoms, number on number.
Mine is the house of the dead which you properly occupy at your ease
Showing it off like a proud owner. A handful of atoms reminisce:
"We were a lock of hair once upon a time." Others remember they
Are bone. You are breathless and confused, the ceiling grows soft
As cheese before your eyes, then, at once, you're pierced with Love
Which wordlessly says within your heartbeat: "You're mine, I'll free
You from the cage of yourself, now!" Be silent, Khusrau, be silent,
Savour this timeless moment, speak no more of longing. Oh my tongue,
Oh how this retiring tongue of mine is made exquisite with your sweetness!

Divan 1515

Passing, passing
The blossom gives way to the fruit;
Both are necessary,
One passes into another.
Bread exists to be broken
To sustain its purpose,
The grape on the vine
Is wine in the making,
Crush it and it comes alive.

Mathnavi I, 2930

Inside me reflecting mirrors,
Reflecting me beyond mincing
Words, not beyond what I know!

Apart from my changing body,
Apart from my invisible spirit
I am a stranger in the ocean
Of my being with no identity.

I am not living, can you sniff
The stink of sludge and decay?

You talk in whispers of my madness,
But look beyond my babbling science
To the asylum of truth, I want to say.

Look at me with my containing head
Topping my dervish cloak, do I remind
You of someone you think you know?
This container holds upside-down with
Swelling joy, a liquid not spilling a drop!
If a precious drop escapes, it falls to God
Becomes fixed like the lacquer of pearls.

I grow like a cloud over that ocean of
Liquid absorbing the vapour into myself.
When the radiance of Shams shines on
Me I grow heavy and rich with longing,
And I rain. Then it's spring time and slender
Lilies rise up like the shape of my tongue.

Divan 1486

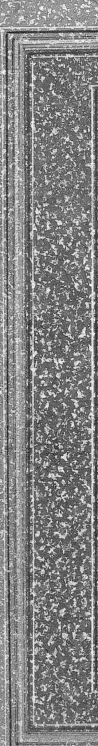

These words of mine are no stones
To pick and throw at passing fancies.
They're yeast-sounds, bread waiting
To be broken whilst they're still fresh.
Leave them overnight and they become
Hard as rusting bolts, not fit for eating.
My verse is harboured in lovers' hearts,
Expose it to the indifferent world
Busy with its traffic and it chokes to death.
Like a fish it swims in the lover's blood,
Land it on the rocks and it gasps for life
Then slowly dies, cold and stiff as an icicle.
You must be rich with metaphors,
Like an ore of gold waiting to be mined
If you are to digest my words
When they're fresh. Know this,
My friend, it's nothing new,
These words are turned to bliss when you
Read them with your own imagining heart.

Divan 981

I was dead, dead, dead
Deep in the basement of darkness,
Then I shot into life.
I was stricken with grief
Pounding my eyes, excavating my heart,
Then I exploded with laughter.
Love vibrated in me
I became the vibration.
Eye-glutted, soul-polished,
My heart is leonine, my being
Bright as Venus.
He said: "You're mild and so reasonable,
You don't belong here."
I left and discovered absurdity,
Became a shackled lunatic.

He said: "You're not drunk, leave this
Place at once. Go, you don't belong
To this brawl of a party."
I left and learnt drunkenness,
I let myself go with delight.

He said: "You've not been slaughtered,
You're not splattered with joy."
I was slain before the sun of his face.

He said: "You're as clever as a monkey,
Juggling greedily with futile notions
And the luxury of doubt."
I became an idiot, impoverished, a loose end.

He said: "You're a light, a niche for prayer."
I'm not a niche, nor light, I'm simply
Choking smoke drifting in the wind.

He said: "You're the Sheikh, the leader,
The string in the labyrinth." I know
I'm none of these, I'm shrinking dust
Blown hither and thither at your command.

He said: "You've the wings of an eagle,
There's no need for me ..."
My yearning for his wings, his airborne form
Grounds me without even a feather.

Quick fortune with tales to tell, entices me:
"Don't take the path, don't be vexed;
I am generous and blessed, I'm your ladder."
Love whispers with slowly fermenting wisdom:
"Remain on my breast, lodge your pulse in me."
I reply: "I'll stay, oh yes I'll stay, my pulse
Is in your hammock; I remain tranquil and in place."

Divan 393

I'm not at home here, here
In this place of distraction.
What am I doing here, how
Did I get on this hard road?
Even a moment, a pinching
Second from the Beloved's
Side is outlawed by Love's code.
If only this strange neighbourhood
Had a hint of him – by God
That would be a feast for me.
How can a finch, the size of
A thumbprint slip away from
This place, even the Simurgh
Proud pilgrim is tied by the foot.
Don't slide my heart, don't
Feint truth, keep your pristine

Place where a column of light
Grows fat on your steady pulse.
Choose a plum flush with golden
Juice rearing life, taste on your
Tongue only the musk of vintage.
Treat aroma, devious image
Playing upside down in the eye,
The cast of colours taking a bow,
For what they are: players, ghosts,
Insubstantial, carping things to
Displace you with shame and strife.
Collect the eye, take a holiday
From your tongue, disestablish
The senses and compose yourself,
For you are pressing on the abyss.

Divan 381

Listen oh listen to my plaintive cry
Listen to my longing or else I die.
From the sweet home of my bed I was torn
So my pain and crucial longing was born.

With so many secrets I sing aloud
But none sees nor hears in this crowd.
Oh for a friend to know my burning state
That our souls may mingle and contemplate.

The flame of Love discourses in me
The wine of Love so enforces me.
Do you wish to know the fire, the flow
Listen my listener then you shall know.

Mathnavi I, I

The moon, O the moon has returned to me
This unique moon is no mere trafficker of light;
It is a creator of fire beyond water's power.
Look at my body's poor leaking shelter, regard
The proper element of my soul, Love has made
The one drunk and has dismantled the other.
When the landlord and my heart sit together
At table, my blood turns to wine, Love cooks
My heart for the feast. The eye is bestowed with
His image. Then I hear a voice cry out: "Like a baton
The cup is raised, the velvet wine is blushing with encores."
Suddenly, my heart is laid open, penetrated by Love
It sees Love's ocean; like a springing gazelle it leaps up
Dancing away to that waiting diamond sea, shouting:
"I can't stay, I must find the way. Come, come now
Follow me!" The sun appears and finds me here waiting
For Shams al-Din's radiant face, and all longing hearts are
Drawn to it like clouds rushing to the midsummer horizon.

Divan 310

Look to the unreaped horizon dancing in this desert of ours,
Our restless hearts, our fitful spirit are fleeting impressions.
Myriad of worlds, place upon place, time in time take shape,
To which do we belong? When you see a man lose his head,
Compelled towards the centre of being, then ask,
Ask him to reveal our secrets, you'll hear from his lips
The hush of our hidden mystery. How would it be if
A discerning ear danced before you speaking the language of
Birds? How would it be if a bird flew up with Solomon's secret
Attached like a licence to its collar? What can I say,
What can I imagine? This story is nowhere to be seen in
The borough of honest knowledge. But there's no way I can
Remain silent as I'm made more compact with distraction.
What sorts of birds, hunter and prey, fly in this mountain air,
In the dancing sun-tipped air of the seventh sky
Where lies my entrance! Let's leave this stuttering story
Too mercurial for daily utterance. Only Salah-al Haq wa'l Din
Can show in the place of fickle words
The terrible, unspeaking beauty of our hidden Lord and Creator.

Divan 239

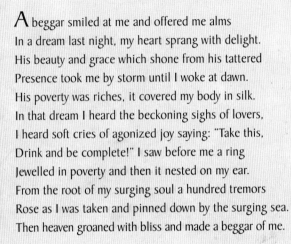

A beggar smiled at me and offered me alms
In a dream last night, my heart sprang with delight.
His beauty and grace which shone from his tattered
Presence took me by storm until I woke at dawn.
His poverty was riches, it covered my body in silk.
In that dream I heard the beckoning sighs of lovers,
I heard soft cries of agonized joy saying: "Take this,
Drink and be complete!" I saw before me a ring
Jewelled in poverty and then it nested on my ear.
From the root of my surging soul a hundred tremors
Rose as I was taken and pinned down by the surging sea.
Then heaven groaned with bliss and made a beggar of me.

Divan 2015

Love is longing and longing, the pain of being parted;
No illness is rich enough for the distress of the heart,
A lover's lament surpasses all other cries of pain.
Love is the royal threshold to God's mystery.
The carnival of small affections and polite attachments
Which litter and consume our passing time
Is no match to Love which pulses behind this play.
It's easy to talk endlessly about Love,
To live Love is to be seized by joy and bewilderment;
Love is not clear-minded, busy with images and argument.
Language is too precocious, too impudent, too sane
To stop the molten lava of Love which churns the blood,
This practising energy burns the tongue to silence;
The knowing pen is disabled, servile paper
Shrivels in the fire of Love. Bald reason too is an ass
Explaining Love, deceived by spoilt lucidity.
Love is dangerous offering no consolation,

Only those who are ravaged by Love know Love,
The sun alone unveils the sun to those who have
The sense to receive the senseless and not turn away.
Cavernous shadows need the light to play but light
And light alone can lead you to the light alone.
Material shadows weigh down your vision with dross,
But the rising sun splits the ashen moon in empty half.
The outer sun is our daily miracle in timely
Birth and death, the inner sun
Dazzles the inner eye in a timeless space.
Our daily sun is but a working star in a galaxy of stars,
Our inner sun is One, the dancing nuance of eternal light.
You must be set alight by the inner sun,
You have to live your Love or else
You'll only end in words.

Mathnavi I, 109

There are times when I seem asleep to you
Without the integrity of faith in this my dreaming state.
But don't be deceived, my eyes are shut but my heart
Is as alert as a deer whilst it drinks from the pool,
My resting body is wired with instinctive energy.
The Prophet said: "My eyes are sleeping but oh
My heart is alight with the Lord of us all."
Your eyes may be open but your heart is sleeping,
My eyes are closed, but my waking heart stands erect
Dawn-fresh before the threshold with its own wakefulness.
My heart's amphibious senses swim in the two worlds
So don't judge me with the disfavour of your weakling will,
Which only sees darkness where I behold the coursing light;
What appears a prison to you is a scented garden to me,
The highest pitch of action is simply repose for me.
Your feet are in the muck, to me that sludge is as a rose.
When you hear the wailing of a funeral, I witness
A whirling dance at a wedding feast; I'm with you on the earth
As earth, but as spirit I'm in the seventh circle of heaven.
I'm only with you in this transient shadow that is my body;
My joy is beyond the cusp of your frantic imagination;
Now I've broken free of the dull gravity of knowledge
I take it and use it and do not let it oppress and abuse me.
Like insects we are trapped in the web of thought,
We are entwined in cords of anguish from moment to moment.
I can visit thought with diplomatic lightness ready and able
To spring away with a flick of a finger from its net when I will.
Thought is my prey waiting for my will, I'm a hunter with a heart.

Mathnavi II, 3547

So deliberate is the power in him
That no grace can escape his shadow.
Don't blame me for his coldness to you.
You moan and groan too easily since
His beauty treated you cruelly.
But when like a colossus he bestrides
Both worlds, he cannot help but be cruel.
His love is enticing even if he
Grants you no compensating kindness.
His beauty is constant even if he acts
With callous rigour on your being.
Show me a place which is not bathed
In his light for proper eyes, a chink in
An edifice which expels his fire with its

Mouldy darkness. The eye and crystal lamp
House complementary light, join them
And no one can split them apart.
The spirit floating calmly on the aether
Says to itself: "Only God can see God
In all God's beauty as a mirror unto God."
But each affirmation is as garrulous
As it is truthful. God is a jealous creator
Moulding His face naming it: "By the Dawn."
Sham's countenance, the sun generating
Our path and place, Pride of Tabriz, gives
Endless life impregnated with his light,
The rest is instant darkness.

Divan 861

From moment to moment the soul
Dies and grows in your presence!
How can any person plead for a single soul?
Your feet are like fecund rain feeding a parched land,
From each footprint a new head springs up
Yearning for you. How can anyone
Take leave of you for a created head?
The moment the pointing soul sniffs your scent
It trembles in anticipation and scrambles towards you.
Once you fade and withdraw, my bewildered mind
Stiffens with grief, sleek hair grows dull and grey
In lamentation for you. My heart is emptied
In readiness for your banquet and the
Exquisite bed on which I may die with joy.
I'm dissolving myself like salt in water
So that you may grow and supplement my being.
My soul, in the churning wake of Shams-e Tabriz,
Steals along the pearling ocean like
A rusting ship without a keel.

Divan 622

Time passes, time passes wearing out all clocks
Travelling into the eye of night. The dance
Of senses is stilled in night prayer
The path to the Unseen unveils itself.
Sleep's angel shepherds its flock of spirits towards
Spectral cities and rose-proofed gardens
Beyond the deadly confinement of place and time.
Now the spirit freed from the cell of the sleeping
Body and the drab images of its daily
Senses, feels with the heart's revealing eye
A thousand forms and shapes, origin of origins,
Of one eternity and unblemished moment.
You could justly say the spirit has come home,
Refreshed and a child again in this shy epiphany.
Its heart now an inner space made clean by contiguous
Forms coating its skin with recovered bliss.

Divan 943

Today and yesterday and unfortunate tomorrow,
And the series of tomorrows allotted us are surely
Dreams, dreaming dreamers dreaming reality.
Time's twilight is closed down by the dawn of death
Tearing us from the illusion of each carping moment
Now that we cease to be dreamers dribbling small daily
Griefs and aches, and enter laughing our keeping home.

Mathnavi IV, 3654

Your beauty is glory in nakedness, the melt
Of smooth skin unsullied with petulant jewels
And the spoiling touch of silk. Your delicate face
Is as pure as the milk of the full moon.
I entangle my limbs with the satin of yours;
Souls without sin, our unspeckled bodies
Are young with the spring of innocence
As we join together to journey
From place through time to eternity.

Mathnavi VI, 4618

I have no idea what makes this heart of mine
Bend itself to you; what is its essence? Is it fire?
Is it water? Is it simply a pumping fist of flesh?
Or is it a stranger, a Peri, an ingenious spirit?
Where is your origin O heart, what is the food you
Thrive on? What makes you so hot for non-being?
Why do you yearn for this ice-pick of Love, for the bliss
Of no-place and no-time? Why, O heart, you who
Are deemed to feed my body and mind, do you look to
Distract me and destroy the order of myself, bring
Shame to thought and tear down your separation?
All living things have more sense than you with
Your partiality for nothingness which draws you
Like a vortex draws the destiny of swirling water.
You are intemperate in your haste, drunk, distracted,
Who will you listen to? How long will you be taken in?
You are a mountain torrent rushing down steep sides

Clambering over rocks with such impetuosity you take
My breath away. Nature and its seasons are too tried by you
To understand your ways; the dew-dressed lily and
The stately cypress bow under your pressure: you are
No common rose, no narcissus of the soil. The tapping
Of the tambourine without the commerce of cymbals,
Like the mad apostate's lunacies, does not enter the custody
Of our ears. Your Moses-love speaks wholly to me and says:
"Become distant, untouchable by the cheap coin of the senses."
How am I not to take flight, to run away from Samiri?
But I have made that beyond-distance, cut a telling measure
Of space even though I live among friends and followers,
I am like the gold Ja'fari coin buried like frozen lightening in the rock,
I may cry out a thousand times: "I am gold!" but no one hears
Until I am mined and minted into a coin of good authority.

Divan 2480

This night of Love
So filled with longing
It contracts my heart
Makes a glass thirsty
For the ruby of your
Wine, then more, then
More from your chastity
Pouring itself into the
Form of this night
Of single pointed joy.
You tease me with
The golden feathers
Of your trembling hands
So intensely light,
I rise up and drink
Your wine, confuse
Myself and emerge
In you, fusing mine
With your own and now
You host yourself.

Ruba'iyat 1878

You're so at home in this passing state,
In the lottery of the here and now,
In slumber you find yourself in another
Space no stranger than the waking place,
Now ill at ease in a forgotten panel of your mind;
You do not say: "What place is this
So strange, so different and yet the same?",
Not at all; the diffident city of sleep
Is as imaginary as that of sullied day.
Is it surprising then that the soul, the inner child,
Which remembers nothing and nothing forgets,
Should not recall its home and birth place when it's
Drugged with body's weight, trawled through
The five-pointed darkness of here and now,
Wrapped like a star in eiderdown?
This innocent traveller enters and passes through
Many states, collecting, like a forgotten
Piece of porcelain, valedictory dust,
How can it review its estate and remember,
When its memory is nothing but rust?

Mathnavi IV, 3628

Stones rush to dance before the
Laughing beauty of your face,
Return from hiding once more
And play like fire on our fickle senses
So we may learn to unlearn and use a pick
To crack the cold glacier of knowledge
Before your dazzling light.
Restore our rusting souls,
Unveil yourself that water may discover
A pearl in your simple reflection,
Fire toy no more with destruction.
Your beauty impales the moon,
Wipes out those indifferent earthly lights
Which hang and wait to be extinguished.
When I'm before your face I have
No time for the peeling mirror
Of ancient heaven's sensual spaces.
You have come and with your sigh
Have created again this narrow world
Now wide and clement as the sky,
Let Venus play her harp to fire and fuse
The solar energy of your loving eye.

Divan 171

I will only to an open heart a story tell,
Listen or your heart shall be lost in hell.
Take heed, attend and you shall know
How blind greed sucks you in its undertow.
Every person whose pox is this sweating sin
Has a miser's heart in deed and thought within.
The lust of possession blinds the heart,
The lust of rank and place keeps you apart,
Like falling hair it robs the eyes of light,
Greed nipples its litter with grasping spite.

Mathnavi II, 578

We are the fingertips of blind illusion,
You are the absolute Cause of causes.
You sing us into being, quick-fading echoes.
We're like heraldic lions on folded flags,
One breath from you and we are unfurled
For a fluttering moment on your dancing breath.

Mathnavi I, 602

When for an infinite second
You leap like an antelope
Out of time's snaking passage
You leave attachment behind,
It fades into the distance.
Timeless, without expectation
You're born into non-attachment.

Mathnavi III, 2075

The Master has been intemperate and ill
Since midnight, he moans and groans and bangs
His head against our wall like a horse with distemper.
The world is weeping with pity for him,
His breaths are like bellows stoking a fire-storm in him.
This is a strange illness, no fever, no ache, no pain,
An illness beyond earth's boundaries, from heaven's navel.
Galen, the physician took his pulse, but he shook his
Enthralled head and said: "Don't waste your time with my wrist,
Explore the entangled garden of my heart,
Use methods finer than your common surface-ways."
He is defiled by none of the antique sicknesses
Neither by black bile nor yellow, nor colic, nor the
Whimsical affliction of dropsy, his illness is beyond
Reason's narrow estate, it hits the headlines with mystery.
Yet he's flush with energy from Love which cares for him

It's bizarre: he doesn't eat, he doesn't sleep
Like a mother. Moved to pity, I say aloud:
"May God grant him relief from this sickness,
He deserves it who has injured no one."
Heaven's reply is equivocal: "There's no remedy,
None that can screen the inspired duplicity of his lover's rage,
He needs not the chains of paltry advice nor morsels of pity,
He has fallen into grace beyond incorrigible piety.
When did you see Love? You have no knowledge
Of its language, so be silent, try none of your cheap charms
Nor the poisonous pharmacy of deceit which is your trade".
Rise up O Shams-e Tabriz rise up, source of light, rise up
And soften the congealed and gelid spirit of your lover with fire.

Divan 321

I said to my heart, this stranger who embellishes me:
"Why do you behave in such an unruly manner?"
My heart replied with silent music:
"Why don't you join me in Love,
Extract the worn-out teeth of words
Become one with delight?" Even if you were
Life-giving water you cannot shun the fire of Love.
You are as sharp as a knife oiled with subtleties,
You are like the restless wind without gravity,
You are seething with images; yet like an unwitting
Mirror you hold the reflection of beauty within this
Stranger your heart. Empty souls reflect
Empty thoughts on others, but you are a
Lamp in the pit of your earth-bound body.
You are as fine as the eyelash of Certainty.
From which mine were you created like a shining ruby?
Now you need to be set in the ring to become
A jewel on the finger of Love.
Your unsheathed anger shall shame
A thousand fertile compassions;
O Shams-e Tabriz how beautiful is your form,
How rich are you in the loam of your being!

Divan 2760

Today I saw clearly that gem, my Beloved, who
With a prophetic leap took hold of the rope to heaven
Like the spirit of Mustapha.
How the sun frowned at his boldness,
It spluttered with the intemperance
Of a clogged heart when it spied his shining face.
His incandescence turns water and dull clay
From objects to glowing slaves of splendour.
I cried out: "Where is the ladder
On which I may climb to heaven?"
He said: "Your head is the rung, place it
At your restless feet, step upon it and you shall step
Upon the head of the stars. Dive upwards
Swim through the air, like this
Take your heart with your head and come!
Now the paths to heaven open up
Like tongues of flame in you, you shall rise,
Rise up to heaven like the silken sounds
Of the faithful during morning prayer."

Divan 19

Your eyes must complete their course of Love
For you to beat a path to courteous truth;
Spend not your time with cold faces in dead places
Or else your breath will freeze your breast and heart.
From the pulp of yearning go beyond its form to seek
More than solace in the natural suffering called Love.
If you're obtuse and heavy as burdened clay enclosed
By gravity, you'll never lift off and circle the sky;
Come as fine as a thousand dancing particles of dust,
So float and find your feet in the silken path of light.
Choose to break or else be broken by the epic
Of your maker; for death will break your fleeting self
Like an empty shell without a pearl. When a leaf
Withers, in season new roots duly restore it green;
Why then flirt with rootless loves
That steal your eyes from the Unseen?

Divan 2865

I am so drunk with the sagacious beauty of your face,
So taken by the intoxicated pupils of your gazing eyes,
O master, so netted my heart, that asylum
Of anxiety and longing, writhes with Love,
There is true affinity between eye and eye of lunatic and drunk.
Take pity on my wasting heart and look on me fondly
As the sun looks with gentle magnanimity on the crumbling
Severance of broken things. Gaze on me
With the spring-season of your eyes
So that oaks may grow from a single acorn.
Your hybrid eyes are concentrated origins
Ready for ecstasy and blood with their fervour.
Those eyes have invaded me and taken
What they will from my heart
So that the bewildered youth runs naked
Here and there in the empty house.
We will enter the garden of your face and abandon the house,
Demolish a thousand like houses with our bare hands
In eager expectation, turning them into powder.
Salah-al-Din you are like a moon without a shadow;
You have no need for this song of mine,
No more the houri's golden hair has of a comb.

Divan 2412

Seek to replace the lead of your eyes
With a living ear which learns to die;
For sacred words too fine to pierce the frost
Of blind hearts, live in hearts with light embossed.
The Devil insinuates the hearts which lie
As crooked feet only crooked shoes try.
You may intone sacred words and ancient sounds
With the mechanical tick of a clock expound;
For a fool words will fall on barren ground
Even if you mint them on the willing page,
Even if you speak them slowly like a sage;
Oh sinner! The devil may take you at your word
But wisdom's too wise by you it's not heard.

Mathnavi II, 315

We speak of God who is hidden
Describing the indescribable.
You philosophize, I only criticize
Another refutes us both.
Yet another,
There are always others,
Will pontificate and vilify
And pin truth down like
A dead butterfly.
Everyone prognosticates
And assassinates with
A knowing word, a nod,
A distant seeking look;
Each insinuates even to
Himself even that he knows.
All these busy mouthing truths
Cannot speak the hidden Truth;
Yet each carries in itself
An antidote for its being
As blindness contains insight,
As the fleeting moment
Unveils eternity. Be patient
With your counterfeit truths,
Like false coins to the real,
Is their value to be measured.
So, like God's word in the Book
We learn to discriminate –
All is not true nor all entirely false –
As a small dose of poison
A potent medicine makes,
So our partial errors our thirst
For impartial Good do slake.

Mathnavi II, 2923

Heart in tumult, our hermit beings blunted with
The rasp of inward noise; here now,
There in tomorrow's heart. Ears stuffed with
Cotton wool, eyes distracted by a single hair
Sharp as a blade of grass. We wait anxiously for
Tears of grief to spill over like lava onto our cheeks.
Let Love invade you and consume that deadening wool,
Let your heart become an audience like Hallaj,
Like the audacious Saints of Purity.
You know what happens if you place a naked flame
By cotton wool, the fire will eat up
Its desiccated convulsions. You are skirting
On the lip of Love so prepare yourself, throw open
The mantle of your senses to joy. For the lover's death
Is a willing return on the way to the One;

If, entangled in the fingers of grief,
You fear death, this is no place for you.
So far as this existence is a prison
Which bricks up our senses,
The destruction of this cell is
Our innocent ambition.
But his prison is like a palace,
His palace is a heaven.
There's no lasting monument in this life
Where even mountains are like balls of cotton
In this faithless circus of passing beauty,
There's no belonging in the hovel
Of space and time, there is no loyalty.

Divan 246

Look! Quickly, look there among the trembling feathers
Of the copper beech, there, you see them – birds making
Ready to ride the dawn skies. They'll rise up soon, rise up
Leave behind their conferring selves, to skim the seventh
Heaven turning and changing with the stripling light,
They're no ants that serve a modest sky, their eggs are golden.
Asleep, they cradle the sun and moon in their folded wings,
When they swish over the face of the waking sky they're fishes
With souls of whales; they're like wild roses dancing in the wind,
They adorn the skies with capricious patterns, wings beating
Like palpitating hearts. They are independent beings, teasing hell,
Skimming heaven, free of blessings and curses they'll lord it
On the day of resurrection they're so close to our handcuffed
Souls no bodies can quite acquit. The bravado of their display,
The swooping dives and daring curves upward to heaven daze
The mountains with subtlety and the sudden converted sea,
Now bitter now sweet; their agile flight refines bodies into indebted
Souls; souls in turn are winnowed through the pale of Eternity;
Dull stones are blooded into rubies and the hollow bones
Of unbelief are filled with the marrow of dancing truth, picking
Its way over the debris of our senses. They're so clear, so finely,
So thrumming fast they're invisible to the eye. If you want to
See them look quickly with your turning heart, powder your face
With the dust from their claws, make ready to go to the ball.
Prepare to blunt the sharp point of your questing mind so it may
Look up into the skies and blossom as rose and eglantine.
Now, if all this could be said, I would say it in such words
That the chorus of angels and caustic jinn who seal our play
Would shake their fiery locks and cusp their hands to pray.

Divan 730

Again with burning lips I swore
An oath in last night's heart,
I confess with a sigh again I swore
An oath on your ruby blood.
I swore that I would fix
My longing gaze on your chaste smile.
I swore that I would not flinch
Even if you struck me with a blade,
My faith in you is green and strong
It would rise again unscathed. I suffer,
My heart is torn from your breast
Which none can cure but you.
You may wilfully cast me into fire
But I am an ingot glowing for you.
I swear I am dust, dry powder
Rising from your path, as hapless atom,
A circling world held by your gravity
I turn and turn in your wake.

Divan 1559

O friend do you see this sky-planted
Tree of knowledge, you who know?
See how high, how generous
The rich tapestry of shade from it flows,
The merciful vein of water as great
As life-giving as pliant as the ocean.
But in your ignorance you see only
The opaque husks, the futile motions
Of forms, for you fail to drink from
The fountain-head of the One; you only see
The names which crush and crowd
The traffic of your senses – sun and tree
Capricious lake dressed in silver, growling clouds
Heavy with thunder – make their entry
As auspicious names, glinting facets
Of the diamond of the One again and again.
Countless words and notions kissing
The fine compliant air like a curtain of rain.
The One may be Father to you, to me Another,
To yet another a new-born Son,
He is Justice and Wrath, Mercy and Vengeance,
Revelation of faith, cherished. He runs
Like a river through the fertile eden

Of particular forms disposing of dancing names,
All this show seems sundry different, contradictory,
Paradoxically it's all the Same;
Made up of a million prancing disruptions
Which our credulous minds deceive
As we chase the froth of names as truth and destination
To the end of life and only believe
In what we see and say, we miss the mark,
The salt which makes us thirst we cannot conceive
Of in what is inconceivable – so why tie yourself
So closely as your blood with seductive labels
Only to be sullied, taken apart, besmirched,
Gulled and clogged like dung-filled stables?
Travel lightly O friend with your enchanted senses,
Take careful stock leaving names behind
So you may be guided to the pity and pith of things
Where resides the One; there your heart you'll find.
We quarrel and coral our faiths in walled enclosures
Of demeaning words, those preposterous names.
But only pierce the surface of your eyes, see
Beyond your blinding sight, bathe in His eternal flame.

Mathnavi II, 3668

Circling, circling like zekr coming and going, circling round and round ...
With all true pilgrims I circle the cause of Love.
I'm not like the sly jackal, ears cocked, sniffling death as it approaches carrion.
I'm a gardener, shovel on shoulder seeking sun-sugared dates,
Striding through thorns
            round and round ...
The fruit I circle and seek is not a dry, acidic pustule on a sour tree,
My dates are brown as honey, they encourage my faithful body
To circle on wings like Taiyar
            round and round ...
The world is a serpent covering a treasure, I float above it
Flickering like a serpent's tail. My grief is not paltry though I wheel slowly
Like a heron about this sacred place
            round and round ...
I do not want to own, to be fluent with worldly goods;
I need the Prince, I long for the solace of his wholeness.

At each waiting moment, Khidr guides my circling feet whirling crazily
Like the lusting needle of a compass seeking true North
            round and round ...
Can't you see I'm ill? I need a Galen for my fermenting mind seeking the vintner.
Don't you realize I'm the sky-hungry Simurgh flying over Qaf
            round and round ...
The hidden treasure, ill-seen ill-sung? Can't you see I cannot stop circling?
Spinning agitation turns me like a top spilling circles on circles, here and there,
            round and round ...
You say: "Slow down now, be more dignified!"
I'm sick of the trick of dignity, I am travelling, yes I am travelling
            round and round ...
In a whirlpool of distraction. Bread is my pretext
The baker my warrant. I'm not measured by the density of gold,
I am inaugurated in my circling
            round and round ...

I have entered the airy, dancing lightness of Love.

Divan 1422

There are so many selves,
So many selves swimming like eels
In the liquid of my mind,
So many fickle impressions.
Which one is me?
Listen to my nonsense, be patient,
Don't try to muzzle my foaming mouth!
I'm not in control, don't plate me in with the glass
Of your comments and easy concern,
I'll shatter and crush it into sand.
I can't help it, I am a cipher for your moods;
When you're filled with joy,
The zero I am is impressed with pleasure;
When you're dark I become dark as a cave.
It's always the same, your bitterness is my brine,
Your sorrow is my fatal grief.
When I am with you I am your lofty sky,
Your placid sea. You're anchored reality,
I am too created in this occupied body.
I am nothing but a mirror in your palm,
Reflecting the play of your fingers.

I take on the skin of your feelings.
You are the cypress in the garden of our being.
I am its obedient shadow;
I am a servant of the rose setting up house beside it.
If I act without you my hands are torn
By thorns, caked with ashes.
With you the thorns and ashes become
Rose petals and jasmine composed with perfume.
At each instant my heart pumps blood for you,
The vessel of my body is fragile crystal for Love of you.
Every second my fingertips stretch out to trace your face
So you may burn my skin, rip open the garments of my soul.
I am a beggar who has received the silver grace
Of Salah-al Din which cools my constricted
Heart like a mountain stream.

He is the light, the glowing flame illuminating the world
But who am I?
From the yearning curvature of my soul
I know I'm simply his bowl.

Divan 1397

You cannot shun sunlight
No more than a suave rose
Survives without its liquid beams.
Plant your inner space with seed
Where feathers of flame play gracefully.
There's something higher we know
But you say not more,
Not this, not that;
I do not know.
You are tied up in *nots*,
But beyond your cautious *nots*
You must see and say what
Really is without not knowing.

Mathnavi VI, 634

When your actions and thoughts strike
That living spark in you, engender your soul,
You work from that subterranean flow of
Joy that runs like a laughing torrent in you.
All other origins bring only dried fruit, no
Love, no energy sinews your emotive being.

Be not made hollow by the noise of others,
Lead by the nose by blind or devious men.
There's one way which leads to the spring,
One rope to use for the bucket to scoop up
Clean water – the trackless way of selflessness.

Be filled with wanton, willing, lusting self
And you are in prison with clipped wings, or
You are a piece of cod sizzling in the pan.

The world grows mad on the ferment
Of angry actions, the authorities can only inflict

Visible punishments. Now regard with the unpractised
Inner eye the unseen presence of Judgement then
You will understand the nature of your soul's torment.

We are like toads croaking in the damp darkness
Of a well, there's no way we can know the vernal
Breath of a sunlit field in this carnal occupation.

Your many selves can point like iron particles drawn
To a magnet, or like the swishing dance of a school of fish
Now this way, now that, move with grace and harmony.

Even a great palace floating like pregnant cumulus in air
With intricate balconies and joining towers washed
By rainwater, with clement infinity sparkling everywhere,
Can be contained in the merciful shade of a single tent.

Mathnavi VI, 3487

Without you I'm entombed,
My flesh rots obediently
And falls away from the bone.
But just your fleeting presence
Brings life to me and fills this
Marginal body with brassy resurrection.
Where you are there is my fragile body
And thirsty soul so longing for you.
I'm a reed waiting, rigid for your breath;
Touch it and you create harmony.
I'm addicted to your play,
An instrument in search for you.
Without you I'm buried in mourning,
Eaten up with grief.

Divan 1641

Don't flounder in the preambles of the past
Wounded with regrets; don't let autumnal
Nostalgia blind you to the sounds and scents
Of the present's Spring; you're a native of
The pellucid moment, make it infinite beyond
The curving snake of passing time and space.
Learn to die in the infinitely elusive moment.

Ruba'iyat (reference unknown)

I was a speck of dust measured in molecules
Now I am a rising mountain peak, snow-capped;
I was forgotten like coffee grains in an empty pot
Now I am surging light leading a multitude.

You erased my famine, unpicked my anger
Your energy charges my voice, it radiates my heart;
Now I am alive with the ore of words pouring
From my lips like molten lava glittering with joy.

Ruba'iyat 1966

Once again to open to the melody
Of the reed of good fortune, listen;
Sing my soul, dance my heart,
Clap your hands and stamp your feet.
The dark shafts of a mine are now glowing
Ruby-red, and the world is festive with welcome,
The table is set for the coming celebrations.
We are drunk on Love, blatant with hope
And adoration of the Beloved's cheek
Fresh as a meadow in spring.
He is the sea, we are the sea mist;
He is the treasure, we are dilapidated beggars;
We are mere hapless particles in the radiant
Light of the sea. I am so amazed, so bemused,
Do not scold me for being boastful,
If only you knew how I am enjoyed
By the Beloved! With the light of Mustapha
I am ready to split the moon.

Divan 2967

SEEKING THE BELOVED

Whirl and rejoice, find the ruby of your heart
Through circling degrees, your body becoming
A planet of the soul embedded in still serenity.
You are your arching senses sending energy
To the centre of the dance; the Beloved calls out
To himself rising like leviathan rejoicing.
Wars are fought here in your dancing blood
Chamber convulsed with joy, it looks upon God
From the famine of its lowly state with longing sighs.
Angels pierce you in your turning with the cool
Needles of their eyes, you are wounded with
Their peace you whirl and rejoice happily drowning
In that enchantment where no body may enter
No sun nor moon, as the dancer brings forth the dance.

- *R. A.*

Index of first lines

Notes about the Poems

p.13: *Mathnavi IV, 733*. Sufism extends and expands the Pythagorean theory of the heavenly music of the spheres to include the human soul. The Sufis maintain that Adam, the progenitor of humankind, heard the heavenly music when he was in Paradise. Henceforth, all human beings have been capable of recognizing that music in their souls, and are drawn by it towards God, the Beloved.

p.14: *Divan 649*. In Persian literature, the full moon is the paradigm of beauty.

p.15: *Divan 2313*. The 'reed of my longing' is a reference to the *nay*, the reed flute used in Sufi music. Its notes are the lamentations of the lover's soul for the Beloved.

pp.16-17: *Divan 2253*. This *ghazal* (lyrical love poem) is about the primordial attraction of the lover to the Beloved. The lover becomes golden from the shining light of the Beloved. The lover has no desire other than to drown in the infinite sea of the Beloved's love. As in the game of polo, though the mallet hits the ball, the ball will always place itself in the centre of the mallet's head.

p.19: *Divan 322*. A description of the mystical union between the souls of the lover and the Beloved. Khorasan in the east and Iraq in the west are used to express a geographical manifestation of this transcendental union.

p.20: *Divan 1919*. In the mystical tradition, madness often symbolizes the dissolving of the self, which in turn opens the mystic's heart to the true experience of Reality.

p.21: *Divan 1254*. Rumi compares himself to a shadow of the Beloved, which he beseeches the Beloved not to cut off. In the Sufi tradition, when a shadow becomes absorbed into the light, it is no longer separated from its source and achieves *baqa*, immortality.

pp.22-23: *Divan 1235*. Rumi compares Shams, a symbol for the Beloved, to the light of a candle in the midst of darkness. His soul yearns for Shams, whose name, like the name of the Beloved, should be repeated by lovers. According to Rumi, kissing the hand of Shams at the point of death sweetens the mouth and removes the bitter taste of death.

p.24: *Ruba'iyat 1879*. The relationship between a true lover and beloved is not time-bound. This relationship, which is simultaneously immanent and transcendent, is a reflection of the eternal relationship between the lover and the Beloved.

p.25: *Mathnavi III, 3808*. For the mystic lover, man-made borders and divisions are meaningless – it is the presence of the Beloved that conveys true meaning to a place. According to Muslim mystical tradition, when Joseph was dropped into a well by his brothers, the rays of light from his beautiful face, representing the beauty of the Beloved, shone like the full moon and lit the dismal well so that it looked like Paradise.

p.27: *Mathnavi II, 1750*. From a famous story in the Mathnavi. One day, Moses heard a shepherd talking to God. The shepherd was a simple man, so he used simple words and simple language. Moses rebuked him for addressing God in this way. The shepherd was heartbroken, but then God called to Moses, telling him that God hears each and every one of God's creatures in the language of their own heart. It is the truth of the heart that matters to God, not the words of the mouth.

pp.28-29: *Divan 1515*. This *ghazal* describes the ecstatic state of the lover at the time of mystical union. The word dervish symbolizes humility and honesty. Here, it is applied to the Beloved. Like the rest of the poem, this verse uses much word play. Khusrau is the name of a legendary

Persian king who was in love with Shirin (literally meaning sweet). Their romance is described in the works of Nizami (a 12th-century Persian poet). The verse is a pun on the name of Shirin: the mystic lover is simultaneously talking about Shirin, the beloved of Khusrau, and *shirin*, the sweetness of the poem's ethos.

p.31: *Mathnavi I, 2930*. The process of transformation in time is as necessary as transformation outside time. One process is temporal, the other eternal; they complement one another. The sweet fruit cannot come into being unless the flower first lives and dies – in the seed lies new life.

pp.32-33: *Divan 1486*. Rumi compares his soul to a mirror reflecting the Truth, which he therefore cannot pretend not to know. For Rumi, Shams is the person who contains the reflection of the Truth, and thus Rumi knows Shams in his soul.

p.35: *Divan 981*. For Sufi poets, words are a part of their life experience – in this case, literally the daily bread which sustains life. The 'bread of Egypt' is probably a reference to the unleavened bread which the Hebrews baked and ate in haste prior to leaving Egypt. Rumi would have known about this from the Qur'anic references to the story of Exodus.

pp.36-37: *Divan 393*. The literary and mystical importance of this poem is the constant contrasting of opposites. The mystic's experience can be expressed only in irrational and antithetical opposites.

pp.38-39: *Divan 381*. Sometimes a seeker takes a wrong turning and follows a false path. Rumi believes that any deviation or distraction from the path of the Beloved is to walk along the dangerous road of destruction of the soul. Yet even the mighty Simurgh, the mythical bird in Persian literature, is sometimes caught in this snare, let alone the insignificant finch. The heart knows that only the world of the Reality has life; everything else is false, fighting against the Truth.

p.41: *Mathnavi I, I*. The opening lines of the Mathnavi. The Persian reed-flute, *nay*, which is often associated with ceremonies of Sufis of the Mawlavi Order, symbolizes the human soul. The soul, like the reed, is full of air but has no sound. But when the reed is emptied of wind, just as the soul is emptied of the self, then the breath of the mystic who longs for the Beloved will fill the reed. It is then that the reed will sing for the Beloved the beautiful melody of the soul of the lover.

p.42: *Divan 310*. In the Sufi tradition, mystical experiences take place in the heart. In this *ghazal*, Rumi's heart is enlightened by Love, and reaches union with the Beloved by throwing itself into the ocean of the mysteries of Love.

p.43: *Divan 239*. Rumi talks of the boundless space of experience, both physical and metaphysical, which a Sufi must go through. He uses the image of a severed head rolling towards the centre of the mystery as the symbol of a lover who is drawn self-less and will-less towards the Beloved. If only the Hoopoe, the bird who was the messenger between Solomon and the Queen of Sheba, would reveal the secret to us. But one needs a discerning ear to understand such a message, the message which is revealed in the seventh heaven. In *The Conference of the Birds* by Attar (a 12th-century Persian poet and mystic), the Hoopoe is the symbol of a spiritual leader. The reference in line 17 is possibly to Salah al-Din Zarkub (d. 1261) who, after the disappearance of Shams, became involved in the spiritual and mystical development of Rumi.

p.45: *Divan 2015*. Poverty of the heart is of great importance in the mystical tradition. It means emptying one's heart and mind of all worldly attachments, thus surrendering oneself totally and freely to God or the Beloved. In the biblical tradition, rings were inserted in the ear as a sign of servitude. Here, the mystic willingly and joyfully accepts the ring of servitude from the Beloved, for in this servitude lies true freedom.

pp.46-47: *Mathnavi I, 109*. Rumi's description of love is a passionate amalgam of human and divine love. To achieve this effect, he combines the word for the sun in Persian (*shams*) with the name of his master and beloved, Shams. The result is that the reader constantly moves between the immanent and the transcendent, the conscious and the trans-conscious.

p.49: *Mathnavi II, 3547*. Rumi explains the difference between consciousness as experienced by the five senses and the esoteric experience that takes place in the heart of a mystic. Though the eyes of a mystic are shut, he or she beholds and discerns with the eye of the heart.

pp.50-51: *Divan 861*. This *ghazal* is about the emanation of the Light from God or the Beloved. The phrase 'By the Dawn' is the first word of Qur'an 93:1 (known as *The Sura of Glorious Morning Light*). This light, the light of the morning sun, is also the esoteric Light of the mystic. In the poem, this mystical Light is extended to the face of Shams, whose name literally means 'the sun'. Thus the metaphor is also a pun on his name.

p.52: *Divan 622*. Rumi begins by stating how life and death continuously follow each other in the domain of God (the Beloved). Yet the mystic lover will not refrain from seeking the Beloved, though this means surrendering life itself. In preparation for union with the Beloved, the lover continuously empties the heart of all phenomena so that it may be filled with the Divine.

p.53: *Divan 943*. Revelatory dreams are important in mysticism, since certain mystical experiences can occur during such dreams. Rumi explains that the spirit, when freed from the burden of daily life's consciousness, can experience the beauty of its original spiritual abode.

p.54: *Mathnavi IV, 3654*. According to Sufis, a person who imagines that this world is the measure of all reality is as misguided as a dreamer who is unaware that he or she is dreaming.

p.55: *Mathnavi VI, 4618*. In the Mathnavi, Rumi puts forward what would have been a daring and almost heretical concept to religious orthodoxy. He suggests that coming to the presence of the Beloved who is clothed in glory and majesty is an inferior experience compared to beholding the Beloved stripped of the veils of these attributes. But a human being can behold the Beloved only when he or she has reached a state of total inner annihilation.

pp.56-57: *Divan 2480*. Rumi questions the essence of the heart. He likens the heart to a person living among a people, but not of that people. Similarly, the soul must free itself from the constraints of the body, because the soul is like a nugget of gold which is not appreciated until mined out of the earth. In the Qur'an, it is said that Samiri was the man who made the golden calf and led the children of Israel to worship it. Moses, who banished him from the camp, told him that his punishment was to become 'untouchable'. Later on, the word 'untouchable' became associated with disease and leprosy.

p.59: *Ruba'iyat 1878*. The word *saqi*, usually translated as 'cup bearer', is a metaphor for the Beloved's continuous emanation. When a person completely empties his or her heart and mind of every thought and feeling not related to the Beloved, then that person will become the container of mystical wine emanated from the Beloved.

p.60: *Mathnavi IV, 3628*. The soul is like a traveller who seeks the perfect city, the city which it will recognize immediately as its city of origin. There is no separation, no isolation, and there are no strangers in that city. There, the soul is re-united with the Beloved.

p.61: *Divan 171*. When the Beloved's divine beauty is revealed, even the inanimate world of stones becomes infused with the ecstasy of love. Nothing can be compared to that beauty, *jamal*. The moon and the sky are but a hanging light and a rusty mirror compared to the beauty of the Beloved.

p.62: *Mathnavi II, 578*. Greed is the darkness which will prevent the eyes and heart of a person from receiving the light of Truth. Though this person possesses all the wealth in the world, he or she will be spiritually empty.

p.64: *Mathnavi I, 602*. Humans might think that they exist, but they are only the non-existent; their being is no more than a breath of wind. The only true existence is the One, the absolute Being, the Divine.

p.65: *Mathnavi III, 2075*. Rumi explains the phenomenon of timelessness as experienced by the mystic. When the metaphorical and mystical leap from material time to non-material time occurs, then the duality of time and non-time vanishes and all that remains is Time.

pp.66-67: *Divan 321*. This *ghazal* describes the outward manifestations of an inner affliction. When a person is truly in love, he or she appears to the common eye to be ill. To the enlightened eye of the mystic, this apparent affliction is in fact a blessing.

p.68: *Divan 2760*. Kohl is a very fine powder, used for beautifying the eye. In the original poem, kohl is used as the symbol of a contrite and humble heart and, by extension, of the mystical experience which takes place in the heart of the lover. It is this which beautifies the eye of Certainty – the absolute knowledge or mystical experience, which is permanent. This is set in contrast to rational knowledge, which is transient. It is acquired by the rational faculty and is subject to change.

p.70: *Divan 19*. Mustafa is one of the prophet Muhammad's names. The Beloved's spiritual ability to experience the Divine is compared to *mi'raj*, the mystic *Vision of Ascension of the Prophet to the Seventh Heaven* (Qur'an 17). The placing of the head upon the feet is a reference to the prostrating posture in Muslim prayer. In orthodox religious understanding, this is how one bows to God. In the mystical tradition, God becomes identified with the Beloved.

p.71: *Divan 2865*. According to the Sufis, one could make the mistake, when looking at beauty, of seeing merely the face or the form. This limited outlook does not enrich the spirit. That is why Rumi explains that the true mystic looks at beauty but sees Beauty. This is the experience that transforms a simple grain of sand into a precious pearl; this is what enables the human to become Human.

p.72: *Divan 2412*. Houri is a nymph and also the virgin of paradise. Salah al-Din is the great Muslim leader of the Crusades, known in English as Saladin.

p.73: *Mathnavi II, 315*. Sufis and jurists often did not see eye to eye about religious matters, and Rumi was no exception. Here he compares the heart of a spiritually ignorant person – though one who is highly educated in worldly subjects – to a deaf ear that cannot hear the Truth, but only distorted sounds.

p.75: *Mathnavi II, 2923*. According to Rumi, all philosophies as well as all religions contain some truth, which is why human beings search for truth in different doctrines and disciplines. Charlatans, in order to gain worldly goods, take advantage of people's gullibility, and portray half-truths as the Truth.

pp.76-77: *Divan 246*. This *ghazal* expresses the difference of perception between the mystic and the non-mystic. For a Sufi, the body is no more than a prison, which must be symbolically set on fire to free the incarcerated spirit. A mystic does not expect faithfulness from this world, because all worldly loyalties are meaningless when compared with the true fidelity between the lover and the Beloved. Hallaj was an iconoclastic Muslim mystic and poet of the 9–10th century.

His unorthodox views on the Unity of Existence with diverse manifestations led to the charge of heresy being brought against him. He was martyred in 922 CE.

p.79: *Divan 730*. In the mystical tradition, birds can represent the soul. Their beauty manifests the beauty and perfection of the soul of the lover. They are the free spirits who move comfortably between heaven and earth.

p.80: *Divan 1559*. In the original Persian, the phrase represented here as 'ruby blood' is 'by your life'. The lover accepts any punishment from the Beloved, even death. In the Sufi tradition, the lover trusts the Beloved totally. The lover rises like a particle of dust out of the path of the Beloved, and willingly returns to dust.

pp.82-83: *Mathnavi II, 3668*. This poem is part of a long section in the Mathnavi on how not to be misled by what outwardly seems to be real knowledge. A king has been searching for the tree of knowledge whose fruit bestows eternal life, but has failed to find it. A Sufi explains that the reason is that he has been looking for the tree rather than for the transcendental meaning of the tree. Those who seek the Beloved in names and concrete terms will fall into confusion and failure. The real seeker must look for inner meanings and through them be guided to true Knowledge.

p.85: *Divan 1422*. *Zekr* literally means remembrance. In Sufism, it is the ceremony in which the 99 Beautiful Names of God are repeated, sometimes accompanied by music. Khezr (in Persian) or Khidr (in Arabic), means green. In the mystical tradition, he is a legendary figure who symbolizes the spirit of renewal, and is the guide of the seeker. Here, the Simurgh symbolizes a spiritual leader and adept mystic. Qaf is the mythical mountain where the Simurgh lives.

pp.86-87: *Divan 1397*. In the mystical tradition, only God or the Beloved has true Existence. All else is a reflection of that true Reality.

p.89: *Mathnavi VI, 634*. The original story in the Mathnavi is about a man, waiting to meet his Beloved, who falls asleep and misses her. Rumi is trying to explain that when people who are too busy negating and denying the Reality are given the chance to experience that Reality, they fall into the abyss of unconsciousness and miss their opportunity.

pp.90-91: *Mathnavi VI, 3487*. This is from the story of Joseph in the Mathnavi, based on Qur'an 12. Joseph spent a long time in prison because, instead of putting his trust in God as the only omnipotence, he asked the butler to plead for him to Pharaoh. The butler, who was not an enlightened mortal and subject to daily cares and preoccupations, forgot all about Joseph. Rumi says that trusting in the power of the transitory world and its people is like asking the blind to lead the blind.

p.93: *Divan 1641*. The life experienced by a mystic separated from the Beloved is akin to death and decay.

p.94: *Ruba'iyat (reference unknown)*. Time is relevant to the world of existence and must be conquered. Timelessness belongs to the world of true Existence.

p.95: *Ruba'iyat 1966*. Here Rumi expresses the belief that the Beloved is the cause of all changes. It is love and service of the Beloved that causes a person, a simple speck of dust, to become like an eternal mountain.

p.96: *Divan 2967*. The splitting of the moon is a reference to Qur'an 54:1. The theme of this *sura* is the final judgement and truth of Revelation. If the moon is split asunder, the end of the world is nigh. Rumi's soul is so elated by the revelation which he has received from the Beloved, that he dares to split the moon, face the final judgement and be joined to the Beloved.

About the Manuscripts

During his life, Jalaluddin Rumi's home city of Konya in Anatolia was an important centre for the production of fine manuscripts. Their quality can be judged from the earliest surviving copy of Rumi's *Mathnavi-e Ma'navi*, which was produced in the city in 1268-9 CE, and which is still preserved there in the museum attached to Rumi's tomb.[1] It would be difficult to find a better example of the supranational character of medieval Islamic culture. The form and style of illumination found in this book was dependent on models developed in the Arab and Iranian lands during the 8th to 12th centuries CE, principally in the context of Koranic manuscripts.[2] Here, though, the book was a work in Persian, recently composed by a poet from what is now part of Afghanistan. The painter responsible for the decoration, Mukhlis ibn Abdallah, called himself al-Hindi, 'the Indian' – and he practised his art in a city that then had a mixed Turkish and Greek population. To a large extent, this supranational artistic unity was maintained throughout the long period when Rumi's works were produced in manuscript. The artistic presentation of these texts certainly changed over time, but a shared heritage and contemporary exchanges between important centres such as Istanbul, Isfahan and Agra preserved many common features.

In Rumi's time, non-figural illumination was the principal form of book painting in the Islamic world and, over the following six hundred years, a great number of manuscripts containing Rumi's works were decorated in this manner. In the beginning, the illuminations incorporated numerous geometric motifs, but this repertory rapidly lost ground to plant-based designs, including arabesques bearing the palmette motif and scrollwork set with fantastic chinoiserie blossoms. The extent of the illumination varied according to the resources of the artist's client, but it usually included an ornamental frame around the opening pages of text. In the grandest manuscripts and albums, there was illumination on every page, and this work came to include decorated margins. These were often painted or dyed in a tone that contrasted with the central area of the page, and then painted with an overlying pattern in gold that was sometimes further enhanced with other colours.

Illumination of this kind can be found in a magnificent 16th-century copy of the *Divan* of Hafiz, several examples of which are reproduced in this book. In these, the only geometric element to have survived is strapwork composed of rotating lobed figures (pp. 25, 54, 65, 94). Floral scrollwork is supplemented here and there by chinoiserie clouds (p. 64), or by cranes and other birds (pp. 24, 55, 58, 59, 68, 69, 95).

Soon after Rumi's death, towards the end of the 13th century CE, non-figural illumination was supplemented by a revival of book illustration, which developed rapidly under the patronage of the newly converted Mongol rulers of Iran and their ministers. The earliest surviving examples of these paintings occur in scientific and historical manuscripts but, from the 14th century, poetic works were also illustrated. Some of these had a strong Sufi content, as demonstrated by the miniature reproduced on page 84, which shows a group of dervishes engaged in an ecstatic dance to the music of a flute and two tambourines.

Where the miniatures were inserted within a narrative text, their content related directly to the story told by the text. An example reproduced here (p. 78) is from the *Mantiq al-Tayr*, or *Conference of the Birds*, by Attar, which was also one of Rumi's sources of inspiration. Another type of painting, the illustrated frontispiece, was more common in manuscripts of lyric verse. It consisted of a painting covering two facing pages, or two matching paintings facing one another, and it always preceded the text. The paintings on pages 58 and 69 form the frontispiece to the Hafiz manuscript mentioned above, while details from two other examples (pp. 12, 97) depict a standard theme for these compositions: a seated prince occupies the place of honour at an alfresco entertainment, which was, we are to understand, the ideal setting for listening to poetry.

Miniatures such as these were created within well-organized scriptoria, in which spare paintings, old cartoons and fragments of calligraphy were kept for reference. On occasion, such material came into the hands of connoisseurs who pasted them in albums. Gradually it became the custom to create drawings, paintings and calligraphic specimens specifically for inclusion in richly illuminated albums. Such album pieces are often in the form of single portraits of types or actual persons (see pp. 30, 40, for example). One group of individuals deemed particularly worthy of such portraits were Sufis, either because of their picturesque appearance or behaviour, or because of their spiritual qualities (see pp. 34, 44, 48, 63, 81, 88, 92).

Youthful beauty, both male and female, was also a subject of these paintings, and in this case the images could be used as aids to contemplation. Rumi believed that human beauty can be appreciated as a metaphor for the absolute beauty of God, and that by gazing at living examples or depictions of them we can gain some understanding of the Divine. The album painting shown on page 34 depicts a young Mevlevi dervish, a follower of Jalaluddin Rumi, and his bland good looks show how the Ottomans visualized this theme around 1600 CE; the youthful courtiers shown on pages 58 and 69 are the product of the Safavid imagination of roughly the same period. Even at this time, four centuries after Rumi's death, a common currency of Islamic aesthetics was maintained in both literature and the visual arts, even if a certain regional diversity influenced their realization.

[1] Zeren Tanindi, *1278 Tarihli En Eski Mesnevi'nin Tezhipleri*, *Kültür ve Sanat*, no.8, Ankara, 1990, pp.17-22. The date in the title is an error.

[2] Mukhlis ibn Abdallah's other known work (Dublin, Chester Beatty Library, ms.1466) is indeed a magnificent Koran manuscript, which he illuminated in Konya in 1278 CE. See David James, *Qur'ans and Bindings from the Chester Beatty Library*, (London), 1980, no.69.

Author Acknowledgments

As with most books, there are many people behind the persona of the author who have helped to bring the book into existence. There is the influence of other writers dead and alive; in my case the presence of Maulana Jalaluddin Rumi pervades every line of the poetry. However, there are people who have had a more immediate influence in the writing of this book. I would like to thank my editor Cathy Fischgrund, for having enough trust in me to commission me; Mehri Niknam, whose knowledge of Persian and familiarity with the poems of Rumi in the original has ensured that the poems I have interpreted are reasonably anchored to the originals; the poet and translator, Jerzy Peterkiewicz, who has given me invaluable help with his instinct for the right word or image; Douglas Krikler for his help and Nahla Nassar for her expertise in finding the illustrative material; and finally Kristine Pommert for her inspired advice and support during the gestation and writing of the poems. Without them this book would not have been written.

Photographic Acknowledgments

For permission to reproduce the paintings on the following pages and for supplying photographs, the Publishers thank:

The Bodleian Library, Oxford:
12, 13 (border): MS.Fraser Add.73, f.1v-2r
78: MS.Elliott Add.246, f.25v
84: MS.Ouseley Add.24, f.119r

Nasser D. Khalili Collection of Islamic Art, London:
front jacket, 96 (border), 97: MSS 712, f.1b
2-3 (border details), 24 (border), 110-111 (border details): MSS 719, f.166b
5 (border detail), 16-17 (border), 32-33 (border), 50-51 (border): MSS 778, f.109b
22–23 (border), 28–29 (border details), 36–37 (border details), 38–39 (border), 46–47 (border details), 56–57 (border details), 66–67 (border details), 76–77 (border), 82-83 (border details), 86–87 (border details), 90-91 (border details): MSS 778, f.110a
14–15 (border), 52–53 (border), 60-61 (border), 70–71 (border): MSS 399, f.2a
18: MSS 913, f.27a
20–21 (border), 72–73 (border): MSS 348, f.484a
25 (border), 65 (border): MSS 719, f.143b
30, 31 (border): MSS 649
34, 35 (border): MSS 505
40, 41 (border), back jacket (detail): MSS 509
42–43 (border): MSS 945, f.2a
44, 45 (border): MSS 997
48, 49 (border): MSS 638
54–55 (border), 94-95 (border): MSS 719, f.128b–129a
58, 59 (border): MSS 719, f.2a
62 (border), 63: MSS 647
64 (border): MSS 719, f.10r
68 (border), 69: MSS 719, f.1b
74: MSS 778, f.58a
80 (border), 81: MSS 650
88, 89 (border): MSS 780
92, 93 (border): MSS 842

V&A Picture Library:
26: MSS 15 13–1962 f.42